D1473323

STORYTIME

SLEEPING BEAUTY

SLEEPING BEAUTY

THIS is the story of a far-off kingdom and of people who lived and things that happened long, long ago.

Among the green valleys of Germany, nestling against the side of a steep hill, there was once a fairytale castle. With flags flying from its turrets and its many windows twinkling in the sun, the castle presented a smiling face to the world. Inside, too, there was music and laughter. For this was the home of a king and his wife, kind and just rulers who were well-loved by all the people of that kingdom.

Yet, in the midst of all this happiness, the queen would sometimes become quiet and her lovely face grow sad.

"For the joy of having a child I would change places with the poorest in the land," she confided one day to her lady-in-waiting as, through her window, she watched the peasant children outside at their carefree play.

The queen's longing was shared by the king. But the years passed and still no heir was born to that kingdom.

Now among the king's subjects were twelve wise women. Nobody knew from whence these women came, but many believed that they were old as time itself and everyone knew that they possessed the powers of magic. One of these women saw with pity the queen's growing sadness and, being a kindly little soul, she decided to grant the queen's wish.

So it came about that, one summer's day, a princess was born.

Such was the joy of the proud parents that they wanted to share their happiness with all their friends and subjects. The king ordered that a great feast should be prepared. Invitations were sent out, and cooks and housemaids and courtiers raced up and down the castle stairs and corridors in a frenzy of preparation.

It was a splendid occasion. All the richest and noblest families in the land attended, filling the great hall with colour and laughter. Present, too, were poor peasants, dressed in their best Sunday clothing, their well-scrubbed faces shining and red. All sat down at the same table and were served with the same food on the king's best gold plates.

From the head of the top table, the king looked round with pleased affection at those who joined with him in celebrating his daughter's birth. His gaze rested with special gratitude on the wise women, seated near him, who would shortly use their wonderful powers to ensure that the life of the young princess was blessed with every grace and good fortune.

One, two, three . . . without knowing why he did it, he counted them. Then an awful realisation came to him. There were only eleven wise women present. Somehow, in

issuing the invitations, he had omitted one of the twelve.

His face paled and his hand, holding a wine-glass, trembled. Then, seeing his dear wife looking at him in concern, he tried to dispel the cold fear that had suddenly gripped his heart.

He would apologise personally to the fairy woman, he told himself, and . . . yes! that was it, he would invite her to another celebration, which would be attended only by his most intimate friends. She would be flattered by this special treatment and would readily forgive the unintentional insult that had occasioned it.

Even as he made these plans the wise women rose from the banquet table. They walked, in single file, to the raised dais on which stood the cradle where the baby princess lay.

Up the three steps went the smallest of the women. More like a farmer's wife than a dainty fairy, she was round and rosy, and her voice, when she spoke, was high and nervous.

"My s-s-sister fairies and I w-wish to bless the ba-by princess at w-w-whose birth we all re-re-rejoice." She pulled a tiny wand from the folds of her gown, and from the wand came great flashes of silver as she waved it over the sleeping child. "I bear the g-gift of love, which she will give and r-r-receive generously."

A second fairy stepped forward. "Beauty of face and form are the gifts I bring. With every year that passes her loveliness will increase."

"She will be graceful as a gazelle, dancing through life on fairy feet," said the third woman.

"Better than beauty or grace, she will have a heart easily stirred to pity for things weak

and suffering, and the desire to improve, by her every deed, the world around her," was the promise of the fourth woman.

Then said the fifth: "The gift of true sight and hearing shall be hers, so that she may see beauty in all things and enjoy the eternal music of the wind and the waves."

"I bring her the gift of laughter which, like the sun's rays, lightens the darkest day." The bearer of this gift smiled down on the sleeping princess.

"Mine is the gift of wisdom, so that she may know the true value of the people and things around her," said a little woman, bent and aged.

The next fairy had a voice that was strong and sweet. "From water, sea and air I give her protection. Neither the fury of the storm nor the consuming heat of the sun will overcome her."

"Riches and wealth will she have, but she will use them wisely for her own happiness and for the good of others," said the ninth woman.

"Joy will be her companion every day that she lives," promised the next fairy.

The eleventh wise woman, the tallest and oldest of them all, began to walk up the steps towards the silk-draped cradle.

But before she could declare her gift a great flash of lightning lit up the windows of the hall, and a storm, more violent than any could remember, raged outside. As though they were indeed expecting another guest, the eyes of everyone present turned towards the heavy oak door. They saw that it had been blown open by a mighty gust of wind, and in the doorway stood the fairy whom nobody had remembered to invite.

She was a tall and stately figure, but her face with distorted and ugly with jealousy and hate.

"So this child is to be blessed above all others, to have beauty and wisdom, wealth and kindness. And joy, too, every day that she lives." The wise woman laughed loudly, and the faces of everyone present grew pale at the sound of that laughter.

"Yes, joy she shall have," continued the woman, "but her days will be few. This is *my* gift to this precious child. In her fifteenth year the king's daughter shall wound herself on a spindle and fall down dead."

In the dreadful silence that followed, the twelfth fairy, who had her gift still to give, bent over the baby's cradle.

"No words of mine can remove this terrible curse," she said sadly. "But with my power of magic I decree that this death which overcomes the king's daughter shall not be a real death, but only a hundred years' deep sleep. This is *my* gift."

The parents of the princess were overcome by dread and sorrow. Thinking to save his dear child from harm, the king sent out an order that every spindle in the kingdom should be burned. That very same evening a mighty holocaust rose up to the heavens as the people gladly complied with the wishes of their king. But the wicked fairy woman only laughed at the sight.

In the years that followed the gifts of the wise women were all fulfilled: for the girl was so beautiful, good, kind, and sensible that nobody who knew her could help loving her. Soon even her parents began to disbelieve that evil could ever befall so favoured a girl. Only her name reminded them of the fairy woman's curse. For she had been called Briar-Rose, and everyone knows that even the most beautiful rose bears a thorn.

The fifteenth birthday of the princess came and went without mishap. Now everyone was convinced that the woman's evil power had been thwarted.

So it was that, a few weeks after her birthday, the princess was left quite alone in the castle while her parents and the servants attended a great function in a nearby kingdom.

The girl was not lonely. She wandered happily through the rooms and chambers, many of which she had never before seen. At last she came to some narrow winding stairs that led up to an old tower. At the top of the steps was a little door, with a rusty key in the lock. When the princess turned the key the door sprang open and there, in a little dusty room, sat an old woman, busily spinning her flax on a spindle.

Briar-Rose had never seen a spindle before
and, being a clever girl, she was fascinated
by anything new.

"What sort of a thing is it that jumps
about so gaily?" she asked the woman.

"Try it for yourself, my dear."

The princess sat down on the little stool.
But she had hardly touched the spindle
before the spell was fulfilled and she pricked
her finger with it.

At the instant she felt the prick she fell
down on the floor and lay in a deep sleep.

But the fairy who had changed the spell of death into one of sleep, and who knew that this accident must happen to the girl, came now with her friends to the little room in the tower. They carried Briar-Rose back to her own bedroom in the castle and laid her gently on the bed.

"Sleep softly, little princess, and dream sweet dreams," said the good and wise woman. "And so that you may not wake to mourn your parents and friends in a strange world, I will give you company in your long sleep."

Even as she spoke, sleep spread over all the castle.

The king and queen, who had just come home and entered the hall, began to go to sleep, and all the courtiers with them. The horses went to sleep in the stables, the dogs in the yard, the doves on the roof, the flies on the wall. Yes, even the fire that was flickering in the hearth grew still and went to sleep. The roast meat stopped spluttering; the maid stopped stirring the soup, sleeping as she stood; and the cook, who was going to give the boy a smart slap because he had forgotten to watch the sauce, let him go and slept. In the castle courtyard the wind was still, and no leaf stirred in the trees that grew there.

Then all around the castle rose a thick hedge of briars. It got higher every year until it surrounded the whole castle and grew up over it, so that nothing more could be seen of the castle on the hill, not even the flag on its roof.

In the farms and villages of the kingdom those who had known and loved the princess grew old and died. Others were born then and they too died, until at last there was nobody alive who could really prove that the castle had ever existed.

But the story was still told of the beautiful sleeping Briar-Rose, and from time to time kings' sons came and tried to get through the hedge and into the castle. But the briars, as though they had hands, clung fast together. The young men were imprisoned in the cruel tangles, and sometimes they could not get out again and they died a wretched death.

At last, after long, long years, a king's son, handsome and brave, came into that country. He listened to the story of the lovely Briar-Rose who lay sleeping in the hidden castle, surrounded by her parents and courtiers, who slept too.

"I will go and see the beautiful princess," declared the prince.

The old men warned him of the peril of the briar hedge and of the many who, in attempting to conquer it, had died sad deaths.

"I am not afraid," said the prince. "No hedge or barrier will keep me from Briar-Rose."

But now the hundred years were over, and the day had come when Briar-Rose was to wake again. So, when the King's son went up to the briars they became, suddenly, just great beautiful flowers that parted, of their own accord, before him and allowed him to pass through unhurt. Behind him they closed together into a green hedge again, neat and low.

In the castle courtyard the prince saw the horses and the mottled hounds as they sprawled, fast asleep; on the roof perched the doves, their heads stuck under their wings. When he entered the castle the flies were sleeping on the wall; in the kitchen the cook still held up his hand as though to hit the boy; and the maid stood sleeping, her hand still poised to stir the big cauldron of soup.

He walked, amazed, through the rooms of sleeping people. In the great hall he found all the courtiers lying at the tables and on the floor, asleep, and on their thrones slept the king and queen.

His footsteps echoed through the silent castle as he climbed the stairs. The bedrooms were all empty . . . until he came to the one where Briar-Rose lay.

The prince held his breath in wonder at her beauty. He could not take his eyes off the girl, who smiled so gently in her sleep. He bent down to kiss her and, just as he touched her with his lips, Briar-Rose awoke.

As Briar-Rose and the prince went downstairs together, the king awoke. The queen and all the courtiers woke up too, rubbing their eyes.

The horses in the courtyard got up and shook themselves; the hounds sprang up and wagged their tails; the doves on the roof pulled out their heads from under their wings and flew away; the flies on the wall began to crawl again; the fire in the kitchen started up with a great blaze to cook the dinner; the maid resumed her stirring of the soup, and the cook gave the boy a great box on the ear, a punishment that he had earned a hundred years before.

Amid scenes of great happiness and splendour, Briar-Rose married the king's son, And they lived happily till their lives' end.

STORYTIME